HALF A TRUTH

An anthology of poems

Susan Bowman

About the author

I have been writing poetry and short stories for as long as I can remember.
I feel blessed in my life; I've been lucky (and unlucky) in love, have been gifted with five children and have never experienced hunger. However, I have suffered many health issues, which I have thankfully recovered from but which have left me with reduced mobility.

I believe all aspects of life are fuel for writing; the good, the bad and the ugly, as I hope my poetry demonstrates.

I live alone very happily, in the Black Country. I'm retired now from medical laboratory work, and after many years as a volunteer counsellor, I'm taking it easy.

I attend writing groups, open mic events for the spoken word and enjoy reading, cinema and theatre as well as spending time with my grandchildren.

Contents
Chapter one - That's life!

Chapter 2 - On Sadness

Come Home
To The Women
Both Sides of the Coin
Life of a Kind
Big Eyes and Empty Bellies
Pain
Bully
The Ballad of CNB
God's Will Be Done

Chapter 3 - Funny Bones

Let's All Go To Aldi
Seaside
Reading Shakespeare on the way
to Stratford-upon-Avon
The Nappies
Shopping Through The Ages
Quinoa
The Days After Christmas
Water
A load Of All Balls

CHAPTER ONE

THAT' LIFE

The Message

The message was simple
come home it said
every ounce of her being
wrapped in those words
a tiny scrap of paper
filled with huge intent
just come home
he walked away
and dropped the tiny scrap
into a nearby bin

Fisherman's Tale

A happy boy though often underfed,
Cycled to the cut with rod on back;
A bottle filled with water and a little bread,
For when the fishermen shared a snack.

And sitting in the rain or sun
Would perch for hours and catching roots
Or sticklebacks, he relished the aching fun
Of disentangling hooks from biting boots.

Then, leaving school too soon,
Always finding the work, he paid his mum
His board and lodging for an overcrowded room.
He longed to escape when the week was done.

The boy a man now and a father too,
Scarce time for idling on the river bank;
Always further jobbing work to do.
His love of life, his happiness levels sank.

Begging time from the family's pull,
The odd day would find him once more,
In silent peace that others would call dull,
With chair, umbrella, tackle, on the shore.

With ageing maturity and sharp wits,
The old man lives his dream and spends his days,
In peaceful pose and calm pursuit he sits,
As precious hours now pass in pleasant haze.

Difference

While two hearts beat as one,
Lying close together;
Me in silks and satin,
Him in leather.

While two souls weep,
My soul cries more.
My angels soothe the pain of love,
His angels keep the football score.

And when the parting comes
And yes, it must.
My energy simply flies away
His turns to dust.

My World Of Colour

White! Bright with promise, wedding gown, wine and roses.
Hospital sheets: baby gro, perfect poses.
Blue sky, boy bootees, bathed in pride,
Scrunched up face; eyes of blue, open wide.

Deceitful eyes; deeper blue, blue with cold and sadness blue,
Change the mood from calm. Little white lies distort the truth.
Eyes turned red by years of tears, looking back,
Change the mood once more-darkest almost black.

And now-the blue outgrown. Boys to men;
Fathers, partial strangers, the cycle begins again;
Partners, wives. While at home,
The brood from my family nest has flown.

Pink! The colour of happiness, fun, girly,
Teenage daughter, sweetly surly.
Pretty in pink, pampered child.
Red! For vitality, shocking and wild.

Then purple, as a nod to age, disguised,
When suddenly I'm old, revised.
People I meet are not surprised,
To see the light gone from my eyes.

Half a Truth

If I tell you half a truth to be kind,
Say you're beautiful although love is blind,
Say you look lovely although you look rough,
Am gentle when I know you've had enough.
If I say darling, no you don't look fat
Always say you look good in that
When your new hairstyle is really awful
And your bleaching trial has gone violent green
And I wonder if that style is lawful
I tell you it's the prettiest I've seen.
Believe that this is just a little fib
I'll tell you just a little lie
It's because I love you very much
I cross my heart and always hope

Mona Lisa

I always wondered about you
enigmatic smiler
sad or bored or plain
in books of art I saw you
and dreamed about the truth
that so beguiled the greatest artist that lived

always knowing I'd meet you
as an interested viewer
tourist or critic or fan
in life I stood before you
and learned the truth
That mesmerised the most disappointed optimist

Foxes

Under the moonlight, vixen prowls
amid the long grass damp with dew.
The quick red fox, no longer fast;
her belly almost dragging on the ground,
heavy with cubs unborn, still,
she obeys their demands for food.

Tired and hungry, steadfast in her search,
looking for rodents on which to feed
And finding none resorts to grubs and slugs.
The odd frog will have to do tonight.
Tomorrow she will have to risk the town
Where she is not welcome but food abounds.

Exhausted now she returns to the den
and there she tries to rest but aggravated by pain,
she shifts and fidgets and in the early hours of morn
with screams and whimpering groans
seven perfect female cubs are born.
She hasn't long to rest before the need for food returns.
With babies suckling at her breast
her empty stomach burns.

Whether or Not

Whether the weather will be nice
Whether or whether not.
Whether there's global warming
Or it's just becoming hot.

Whether the Russians are at it
With some dastardly plot
About to bring our downfall
Or maybe not.

Whether the crazy president
Who lives in the big white place
Pushes a big red button
Merely to save face.

And whether the seas run dry
Or plastics flood the land
Whether we are responsible
Will we ever understand?

Whether we take control
Or give up the power we've got
Whether the planet survives us
Probably not!

That's Life

It is fire, it is ice
It's hot or cold.
It's beauty and the beast,
It's growing old.
It's love and hate and pity,
It's ugly and it's pretty,
It's a secret never to be told.

It is youth, it is age
Man and child,
It's evil and it's lovely
And it's wild,
It is land and sea and shore,
It is less or it is more
It is gentle and it's very, very mild.

It is narrow,
Short or long,
Enormous or petite,
Weak or strong.
It is lived and loved and lost
Cheap or of great cost
But it is only cherished when it is gone.

Health

Of all the gifts our world bestows,
Of all the joys it brings,
Food and wine and happiness,
Love and special things;
The sunshine and the raindrops,
The snow for kids to play,
And perfect days like Christmas
And the restful holiday.

To chat with friends and loved ones,
To cuddle babies fair;
To cherish precious moments,
To live without a care.
These things give life their value,
Not material wealth-
The things that money cannot buy,
And best, the sacred health.

Autumn

Foggy morning and afternoon,
watery sun creeps past
hanging low like lead balloon,
melting patterns on frosty glass
that chills our faces as we peer
to welcome the winter drawing near.

Love?

By what scale measure love
By which rule can it be
That you can measure minuscule
And I enormity?

VISION

Begin anew.
As before
replenish earth.
The beautiful will remain
reflected in the light
of the life giving sun;
the greens and blues,
the perfumed flowers
and trees with fruit.
The rivers,
oceans wide.
Mountains white with snow.
Forests too, jungles,
wild with growth.
Animals, myriad hues,
and fish to swim
in pools reflecting
the moon at night.
A sky filled
with burning stars
to guide the way.
For nobody.

CHAPTER 2

ON SADNESS

COME HOME

It came in the post
at last
with a clatter and a drop
from the past.
The white and the black
jagged hand
cold and stark
the demand.
No dear or darling
still the tone
no love no kisses
just come home.

To The Women

We should remember when autumn leaves fall,
Those who sadly passed and those who survive.
We remind the females of the world, all
Check your body monthly to stay alive.
Remind the the women this is not a game.
Teach them how to stay healthily untouched
By heinous demons wearing cancer's name.
To check your breasts it does not take too much.
So wear pink and sing and happily dance!
Sisters, live your life to the full extent.
Don't ignore my song, don't leave it to chance;
It is with experience that I vent.
I'm a survivor, so I'm here to tell,
But be assured, I have journeyed through hell.

Both Sides of The Coin

In the mud and the blood and the battle cry
Come the sounds of a soldier lain down to die,
'As God is my witness, I pray to thee,
bring freedom and strength to my people.' quoth he,
'Deliver your children from battle and pain,
that the land of our father we might regain.
In the name of the lord, our flag unfold,
for the sake of Europe: red, black and gold.'

And over the gap which is called No Man's Land,
A young unknown soldier, with gun in hand,
Lies dying in wonder that God could not see,
England and allies as they fight to be free.
He gets to his knees and the prayer he'll make
Is for England and freedom, for democracy's sake.
And just at that moment as he kneels on the ground,
A grenade blows his legs off and he dies with no sound.

Life of a Kind

In stockinged feet and hospital gowns,
White haired from worry, grey from age,
Faces etched with concentrated frowns.
Their pain a self tormented cage.

The daily trudge, the stress,
To dress, undress and pose,
While radiation burns redress
The cruel waste of those.

All kinds of human life is here,
Woman, man and child.
For this is hope and this is fear,
It's life without the wild.

-Reflecting on my days in radiotherapy-

Big Eyes and Empty Bellies

Big eyes and empty bellies,
Scabs and sores and flies galore,
Dusty roads that lead to famine
And war and war, and war.

Babies clinging to empty flesh,
Too weak to wail, too sick to cry,
Expressionless mothers afraid to hope;
Too tired to live - afraid to die.

And then the aid; the trucks, the planes.
The white man cometh to save them all,
He brings not rice, nor seed, or grain,
He sells their souls for the weapons of war.

And in an office a fat man sits,
Not white but black as they.
He deals in death and misery,
He gets a good days pay.

Across the world a mother sees
Distressed, she cannot look,
But vows to send a cheque tomorrow,
Turns off the TV and reads a book.

-The 'Biblical famine' in Ethiopia -

Pain

It's a big black hole that swallows me
And a gnawing at my brain,
And a million hands clawing me
This incredibly evil pain.

It's a deep, dark chasm
And I'm falling in again.
Fighting for my sanity
To escape this wicked pain.

It's a thousand screaming voices in my head.
And the knowledge that I will go insane.
Perhaps it would be better to be dead,
To leave behind this agonising pain.

It's exhaustion, weakness, giving in.
And as my strength begins to drain,
The big black hole offers consolation
And an exit from this world of pain.

- Contemplating suicide during a cluster headache attack -

Bully

Susan Hancock has red hair,
Stephen Jones a limp
While Alan Smith wears callipers
And William West's a wimp.

Michael Miller has spots
And Sharon Johnson smells.
While Adrian Norton is stupid,
Mathew Jenkins always tells.

Specky 'Four Eyes' Thompson,
So blind can hardly see,
And stinky Robert Parkinson
Always reeks of pee.

Tony Wright wears Dunlop trainers
And Jonny wears Woolworths pumps,
Sandra James has impetigo
And always picks the bumps.

Nigel's dad is an alchy
Tom has a junkie dad.
Nora's mum was locked away
Because she was quite mad.

Lenny has hair like a gollywog,
And Imran has curry for tea.
While Lisa-Lee has slitty eyes
Don't know how she'll see.

All the little people
Lined up by the shed
Fifty bullets in my gun
Bang, bang - you're dead.
-Reflections on the damage done by bullying behaviour-

The Ballad of CNB

He was a man with the darkest past,
Grown from the dirt and the murk,
Whose parents didn't give a damn
When discipline didn't work.

He was rough and he ploughed through life,
And he took what he needed to take.
But he started to look for a wife,
And that was his biggest mistake.

He'd always been in charge,
And expected to rule his lady,
Controlling and giving it large.
Best to give her a baby.

Then he told her how to live,
'Do this and don't confess,
Wear this, eat that and never give,
A thought to your happiness'

He bullied and fought and he bore
On her personality,
Until the only thing keeping her going
Was a longing to be set free.

One night the man hurt the lady
In the most intimate way.
And while he was holding their baby,
Told her there was no going away.

Now, the girl was made of strong stuff,
She knew that she was strong,
And although he could get rough,
She knew he was in the wrong.

So she called the local police
And they listened to her tale,
And they helped her to form a case,
So that he could be put in jail.

Now thanks to that brave young woman,
Last week the man was in dock.
The judge gave him four years
Inside, behind key and lock.

And the woman? I hear you ask
That brave girl, my daughter,
Who brought the bad man to task
In the court like a lamb to the slaughter.

She's living now free from fear
She feels as if she is flying.
And we all shed a tear,
But tears of joy we were crying.

Made public by my daughter to help other women

God's Will Be Done?

An angel came down from from heaven one day,
God sent him to take a look.
The angel was shocked at the things he found,
And his wings were splattered with blood and muck.

He called upon God on his private line,
And he tried to describe what he saw,
'Man fighting man, and blowing him up'
He told God, 'I can bear it no more.'

But God told the angel to try to find,
The reason for mankind's hate.
The angel, (dressed in soldier's attire)
Stood in the mud and hoped that it wasn't too late.

And the bullets came and the blood,
So the angel called God again.
'I don't get it God,' he said out loud,
'So much bloodshed and so much pain.'

The angel was saddened by what he knew
And he sank to his knees to implore,
'All this hate and waste of precious life,
I really can stand it no more.'

God was angered by the angel's news.
'You don't need to see anymore,' said God,
'Mankind will learn from the painful mistakes
And lay poppies not blood upon the sod.'

'When this day is over and Earth turns red,
When the loss is counted, and the cause,
And the people remember the glorious dead,
This will be the war to end all wars.'

CHAPTER 3

FUNNY BONES

Let's All Go To Aldi

Let's all go to Aldi,
Fetch a bottle of wine,
A baby bath, a stuffed giraffe,
A plastic washing line.

A guest bed,
A garden shed,
A pair of workman's shoes.
A slab of cheese,
Calabrese.
And some cleaner for the loos.

A pint of milk,
A yard of silk.
A chicken for your dinner.
Spuds to roast, bread to toast,
And a pot of paint thinner.

A cream cake,
Milkshake.
A pretty Easter bonnet,
A snow sled, a kiddies bed,
A card with a sonnet.

Christmas lights,
A pair of tights.
A pumpkin to scare the kids.
Treacle pud, a shirt stud.
Tupperware with a lid.

Everyday's an adventure,
You don't know what you'll see.
Bargains galore, in every store,
An exciting place to be.

- What an exciting new shopping experience was had at Aldi -

Seaside

How we love the seaside;
The sparkle in the light.
The lapping energy of errant waves,
And sounds of surging in the night.

The icy feel on brave toes
As we jump up with glee.
We wonder where it all goes,
When we go home for tea.

Reading Shakespeare While Travelling To
Stratford-Upon-Avon

'This train is for Stratford-Upon-Avon'
Interspersed, this landscape shared with Shakespeare,
brings the bard to life. Poor Yorick, in esteem held high.
Once more into the breach, dear friends,
but all is well that in this good night ends.
See, Kate circles around her love, for his perusal
in a coil of swirly skirts and lacy petticoats,
with much ado made by the notes
as minstrels play and playful jester's tales denote.
'This train is for Stratford-Upon-Avon'
As you like it, so the fields of Warwickshire
speed by like a tempest in the night,
and measure for measure, so each delight
assails the sight, forsooth, the bard is by!
'This train is for Stratford...'
and closing my eyes, thus my ears
against the cacophony;
the weight of such responsibility, to tell to thee,
The glorious words to those who will not see.
I offer penance to the bard for him being unloved.
Yet, when midsummer dreams dance and give
life to the king and queen of the faeries and the ass,
the cold of twelve Christmas nights shall pass,
all come to life in this wonderful place, arrived at last:
Stratford-Upon-Avon.

The Nappies

I wondered down the garden path,
Past fence and privet, pond and trees,
When all at once I caught the sight,
One hundred nappies holding tight,
Flying and dancing on the breeze.

Caught on branches, twisting free,
Dragging and pulling determinedly,
White as light and fresh as air,
Nothing but nappies everywhere.

Torn and tattered, smart and new,
They tugged and pulled and fought with glee.
Their play and pleasure, beyond all measure,
Their bright delight a joy to see.

Now, when the rain clouds gather in the sky,
I look upon that inward eye
. that carries me to a place and time
to watch those nappies as they fly,
fluttering and dancing on the line.

A common sight in the 70's
(With apologies to William Wordsworth)

Shopping Through The Ages

It's Locarno on a Saturday night,
You got to dress the part just right.
Search awhile, act with guile,
Shop 'til you drop,
Get the style.

Buy a length of fabric
To make a skirt,
Go down town to C&A
To buy a frilly shirt,
Wide brimmed hat, nylon Mac,
Heels too tall,
Rum and coke, rolled up smoke,
Queen of the dance hall.

In the 80's you're buying bigger things;
The first motor, wedding rings.
Deposit down on your place:
Habitat orange table, Jasper Conrad label,
Trying your best to fit the face.

Wages stretched forever,
Furniture on the never-never,
Telly from Radio Rental.
Keeping up with the Jones's made you mental.
Pies in tins, nappy pins,
Sofas made from plastic leather.

Kinky boots, dyed roots,
Eyelashes inches long.
Drone on, earphones 'pon
Gilbert O'Sullivan's
Latest song.

We seemed to have it all,
But we worked when we were able.
Spend a bit, save a bit,
Put the board upon the table.

Plenty to eat and drink,
Out on a Saturday night.
A week away 18-30,
If you could afford the flight.

Now the kids don't have a chance,
Poverty isn't funny.
And too many old folks can't manage
On too little money.

Life is a struggle for many,
There's a shortage of happiness.
Some folks don't have any
And some have even less

I guess that we were lucky,
I remember having a ball.
I remember Thatcher's children
Were told they could have it all.

But the sky fell in on the bankers
While the fat cats were getting rich.
All the money's gone to the wankers,
And shopping's become a bitch.

Thank goodness for the charities;
With shops on the high street.
So, while buying all the second hand clothes
We can still afford to eat.

Quinoa

I'm not keen on quinoa
It isn't very nice
I add it to my couscous, and I add it to my rice
I add in nuts and raisins
Grapes and apples too
But it still tastes quite disgusting
Although they say it's good for you.
I'm just not keen on Quinoa,
It tastes a bit like scum
So I put it in the waste bin
And hope the dustmen come.

The days after Christmas

In the days coming after Christmas
when the fridge is quite deplete,
and the chocolate box is empty
save for one lonely sweet,
and the turkey is just a memory
along with the Christmas pud.
We vow to begin a diet
because it would do some good.
But promises are broken
and detox is a difficult thing
especially when we have to begin feasting
when the new year bells do ring.
So save your good intentions
until after the season of cheer
because you'll have lots of time to break them
all through the coming year.

Water

This wet stuff, here, I cannot hold
that trickles like no other.
That forms In nimbostratus cloud
and looks not like another.

The life juice, literally, of living things,
the master of our land,
and maybe other worlds besides
all those we understand.

Each day for granted, we dispose,
as if it were not good,
to drain away in gullies
though precious as life's blood.

Yet, what it is, I have no clue!
What makes it wet I can but guess,
yes hydrogen and oxygen,
but more than that I can't confess.

And even that is not the truth
for some of it is hard as ice
and some of it is gaseous,
and some be frozen twice.

The mystery of water,
This beauteous, wondrous stuff,
this giver of life, this mystery,
to whom words are not enough.

So when you hold a cupful
and sip to quench your thirst,
admire the bounty held aloft,
And wonder, who peed it first.

A load of old balls

What's all this about men and their balls?
The big ones, the medium, the small,
A game's not a game where a Man's concerned
Unless it involves a ball.

There are oval balls for rugby,
For football the thing is round,
For squash it's hard as it could be
And it makes a whooshing sound.

There's a plethora of balls in snooker,
The colours have a different score,
But if the white ball follows the black in
The player must forfeit a four.

For the game of table tennis
Otherwise known as ping-pong,
A ping, then a pong is a good thing
But a pong with a ping is just wrong.

In the summer the game before tea
Is played with a bat and a wicket,
Slow moving and ever so twee,
Because anything else isn't cricket.

In golf the ball's hard and it's fast
One minute it's there-then it's gone.
They aim for the nicely cut grass,
Because sometimes there's a hole in one!

For us girls these balls are old tosh!
For the men it's an important match,
And whether they won or they lost,
They'll always have something to scratch!

9 7 9 8 6 3 8 4 2 7 0 8 5